Ella Bella Coccinella

Written by Erika Ebbel Angle, Ph.D. and Anne Holt
Illustrated by Anne Holt

Coccinella
Publishing

Published by Coccinella Publishing, LLC, 135 South Road, Bedford, MA 01730

Coccinella Publishing is distributed to the trade by Atlas Books

ISBN 978-0-9899953-0-6

Library of Congress Control Number: 2014934581

Printed in the United States

www.ellabellacoccinella.com

For our friends, family, and
inquisitive children everywhere

Meet Ella Bella Coccinella, a very special ladybug.

Welcome to her garden home, full of sweet-smelling flowers and tasty vegetables.

THE Cabbage Cottage

Ella Bella is a happy ladybug. She does what ladybugs do.

Until one day...

She woke up to find her garden **squished!**

Ella Bella tried to clean her home, but...

every day the pile got bigger and smellier!

I need help!

Ella Bella called her best friend, Simon the Robot.

"What's a litter bug?" asked Ella Bella.

"According to my database,"
Simon explained," a litter bug is
a person who carelessly drops
trash and doesn't remember to
pick up after themselves."

Ella Bella and Simon asked the ants to come and help

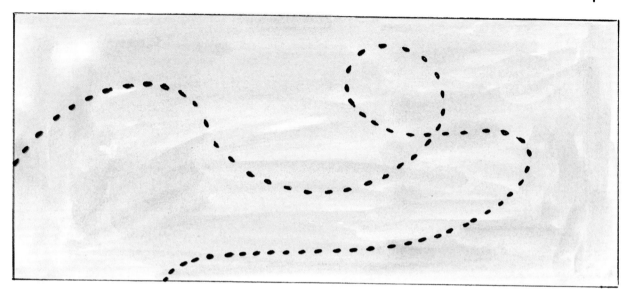

carry away all of the smelly trash left by the litter bugs.

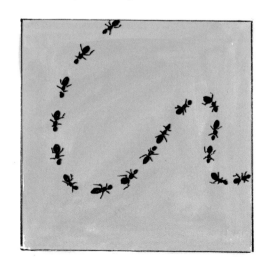

"We need to tell everyone," said Simon.
"We need a bigger team!"

Ella Bella knew just
what to do.

She sent out a message
to all of her friends
and gave them
an important
mission.

Bug Facts
Insect-ionary

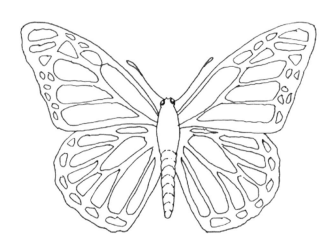

Butterfly

Scientific Name: *Rhopalocera*
Where they live: All continents except Antarctica
Habitat: Everywhere from tropical forest to grassland to tundra
Size: From less than 1 inch to 11 inches across

What they eat: Butterflies sip nectar, sap, and juice from fruits (caterpillars eat leaves).

Other fun facts:

- A butterfly's life cycle has four parts: egg, larva (caterpillar), pupa and adult.
- Butterflies taste with their feet.
- There are more than 15,000 species of butterflies.

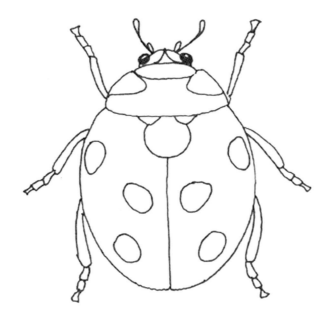

Ladybug

Scientific Name: *Coccinellidae*
Where they live: North, Central and South America, Africa, Europe and Asia
Habitat: Forests, meadows, weed patches and gardens
Size: About the size of a pinky fingernail
What they eat: Aphids, fruit flies, other small insects
Other fun facts:

- An adult ladybug may eat up to 75 aphids per day.
- There are around 5,000 kinds of ladybugs worldwide.
- If bothered, they can release a bad-smelling chemical from their legs to scare away predators.

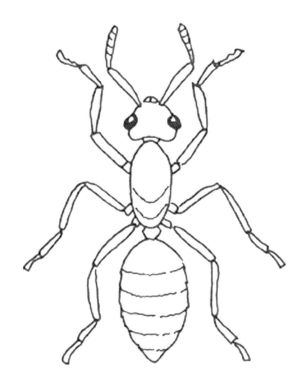

Ant

Scientific Name: *Formicidae*

Where they live: Everywhere except Antarctica and Greenland

Habitat: Everywhere, but especially prevalent in tropical forests

Size: 0.8 to 1 inch long

What they eat: Predominantly plants, sometimes fungus

Other fun facts:

- Ants have six legs.

- An ant can lift 20 times its own body weight.

- There are more than 10,000 species of ants worldwide.

- Ants have two stomachs, one for their own food and one to
  share food with others.

Aphid

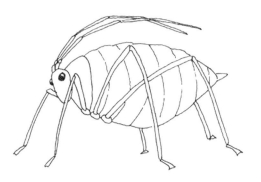

Scientific Name: *Aphidoidae*
Where they live: All continents except Antarctica
Habitat: Almost always found on or near plants, their food source
Size: Very small, only a few millimeters long
What they eat: Various plants
Other fun facts:

- They are often green, but can also be red, black or brown in color.
- Aphids live a few weeks to a few months.
- Aphids are often found in groups.

Earthworm

Scientific Name: *Lumbricidae*
Where they live: Europe, North America and Western Asia
Habitat: Found in soil
Size: From 7-35 centimeters in length
What they eat: Earthworms consume soil as they burrow, extracting nutrients from decomposing things like leaves and roots.
Other fun fact:

- Earthworms are important to soil health because they transport nutrients and minerals from below to the surface via their waste.

Learn more about the insects in
this book at these sources:

kids.sandiegozoo.org
sciencekids.co.nz
biokids.umich.edu
nationalgeographic.com